FERDINAND
WITH THE **EXTRA TOES**
MEETS PETUNIA!!

KATIE MASKEY
WITH ILLUSTRATIONS BY
ASHLEY THOREEN

Ferdinand could barely contain his excitement as he sat looking out the window. The day was finally here! He was going to visit the farm down the road.

Ferdinand had heard about the different animals there and couldn't wait to meet them.

He headed out on his adventure.

On the way, he passed by his old friends Whiskers, Daisy, and Bear. They asked where he was going. Ferdinand proudly told them what he was up to.

Finally, he arrived.

This place was huge! Ferdinand didn't know where to start, but he was off to explore.

That's when Ferdinand saw another animal sitting alone under a tree. He wasn't sure what it was, though. He hurried over to the interesting creature.

The animal was large and round.

It was a light gray color, with dark spots.

"Hi!" Ferdinand said, "I'm Ferdinand, what's your name? Do you want to be my friend?"

But the animal grunted and walked away.

Ferdinand followed, asking lots of questions.

"Excuse me, what kind of animal are you?" Ferdinand asked while trying to get a good look. "Well, I'm a cat," he said, when the animal didn't reply. "I have extra toes that make me special!"

Not wanting to be bothered, the animal snorted and grumbled, "I'm a pig, kid. The name is Petunia and there's nothin' special about me. Now please, leave me alone. I'm trying to find my apple."

A PIG?!

Ferdinand had never met a pig before!

He wanted to learn all about Petunia, so he decided to help her search for the missing apple.

After a few minutes, Petunia moaned. In a grouchy voice, she told Ferdinand how she had lost her apple and couldn't find it because she didn't see very well.

She was sad and ready to give up.

Ferdinand wanted to help. If she couldn't see where the apple went, how would she find it?

That's when he looked at Petunia's nose. It was very different than the other animals on the farm.

Ferdinand saw that Petunia's nose was big, with a flat end and two large holes. Perfect for smelling. He thought about all of the scents this pig would be able to smell—things nobody else could.

"Have you tried searching with your nose?" Ferdinand asked. "It's a really special nose!"

Petunia perked up. "You think my nose is special?"

Nobody had ever told her that before, so she never thought it was important. She took a deep breath, put her nose to the ground and started sniffing the grass and flowers around her.

"There!" Petunia pointed to a pile of dirt with her nose. Ferdinand knew just what to do! He used his unique feet to dig and dig until something bright red appeared. At last, Petunia found the apple with her special nose!

Petunia was feeling much happier. She had never thought there was anything special about her ... until now.

Ferdinand looked at her and said, "Sometimes you just need someone to remind you about how amazing you really are!"

Petunia smiled and wiggled her big nose as Ferdinand scurried away, so happy after his big trip to the farm.

Katie Maskey is proud to share the story of her real cat, Ferdinand, who does indeed have extra toes! Ferdinand is a **polydactyl cat**, meaning he was born with extra claws on all of his paws. Seeing Ferdinand as a special cat inspired Katie to write his stories to remind readers that **you are prefect just the way you are**. In the original book, *Ferdinand with the Extra Toes*, Katie and Ferdinand encouraged children to embrace their own unique traits and to show others why it's good to be different! Katie's mission is to continue to share stories of self-love and acceptance through the adventures of her curious little black cat.

"Don't ever be afraid to stand out from the crowd. You, *yes you*, can inspire others just by being who you are and showing the world your uniqueness." —KATIE MASKEY

Ashley Thoreen is an Ohio-based autism mom and tattoo artist. Her experience in the special education realm not only stems from her role as Parent Mentor for a local school district, but as the mother of a loving 10-year-old son with autism. When not illustrating books, Ashley spends most of her time working with parents and tattooing the masses in a locally-owned tattoo studio (Ashley enjoys creating custom pieces of artwork, whether it's painting or tattooing).

"No disability is a limit, it's a special ability that makes each child unique, our job as parents is to foster those abilities and cherish each day as we learn and grow." —ASHLEY THOREEN

PETUNIA is a real life grumpy pig who lives in Rossford, Ohio. In the summer you can find her sun bathing, in the fall eating all the apples and pears that fall from the trees in her yard, in the winter she takes sleeps like a hibernating bear under her warm blankets, and in the spring she loves rolling around in the mud puddles made from April showers.

Thank you to the Martin family for letting us share Petunia in the story!

FERDINAND is a real life curious cat who was adopted from the Toledo Humane Society and now lives in Lambertville, Michigan. He does have extra toes—three extra on his front paws and one extra on each of his back paws. He loves looking out the windows, chasing his cat siblings around the house, joining in virtual book readings, and snuggling with his humans.

To all of the readers who have supported *Ferdinand with the Extra Toes*, thank **YOU** for being **extra special**.

Copyright © Katie Maskey 2020
All rights reserved

ISBN 978-1-7362105-6-7 (paperback)
ISBN 978-1-7362105-5-0 (hardcover)

Green Clover Books
greencloverbooks.com
instagram.com/ferdinandwiththeextratoes

FOLLOW Ferdinand on social media
@ferdinandwiththeextratoes

Made in the USA
Monee, IL
17 November 2021